THE WORRIES

LEO SAYS GOODBYE

Written and illustrated by

JION SHEIBANI

PUFFIN

Chapter

Leo had always been a very happy boy. He would bounce around rooms doing cartwheels and handstands, energy fizzing through his body like **popping candy**.

1

He also had a huge, beaming smile, which his mum said could **light up** a room.

Lately though, Leo didn't want to bounce around rooms or smile his beautiful smile. Sometimes, he would suddenly want to be alone and still and let his face look . . . **SAD.**

This feeling began a few months ago, after his Nana died.

Nana had been a **REALLY IMPORTANT** part of Leo's life. She looked after him every week when Mum and Dad were at work. She lived so close that Leo could visit whenever he wanted.

And then one day, she was **GONE.**

Nana hadn't been very well. Dad said death happened to people when they got older, and it wasn't something Leo should worry about. He said that Nana had been **lucky**, because she'd had a **wonderful** life and she'd felt ready for it to end.

Leo didn't feel like it was lucky though. It seemed to him that lots of people got ill, but they were OK. So why couldn't Nana have got better?

Leo couldn't even go and visit her flat any more because new people had moved in. Sometimes he and Mum and Dad would cycle past it though, and he'd wonder who lived there now.

Mum said it was normal that Leo still felt

sad. She said his feelings would get easier

with time. But Leo didn't *feel* normal.

And his feelings didn't seem to be

getting easier **at all.**

He found
it hard to
concentrate
at school.

Or enjoy his hobbies.

Or even play with his friends.

Leo seemed to be feeling **worse** . . .

. . . and **worse** . . .

. . . until one day, he had a visitor.

Chapter 2

The visitor appeared, of all places, in his tuna-mayonnaise sandwich, one sunny Saturday lunchtime.

Leo was about to take a massive bite when he heard a frantic voice.

"HEY! NO! **STOP!** HELP!"

"Whoa! What is THAT?!" Leo gasped.

Two huge eyes were staring back at him
from under a slice of cucumber.

"Oh, thank goodness!" The visitor
sighed, wiping tuna mayo off his furry face.
"I've been trying to get your attention for
some time now. This was a last resort, but
I figured your sandwich would be the best
place. You take your food very seriously, kid!"

"But you could've been eaten!" Leo said.

The creature shrugged and raised his
furry eyebrows.

"All in a day's work. So, look – I'm **GRIEF**, one of your Worries. Nice to meet you, *finally*! I was getting so bored in that head of yours, going round and round and round . . ."

Leo didn't know what to say. Surely this must all be a very odd dream? He whispered the Worry's name to himself until it sounded even stranger.

"Grief . . . Grief . . . Grief?"

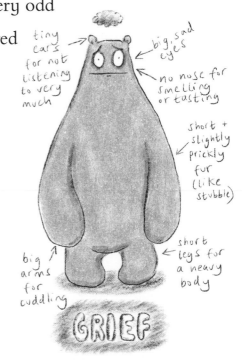

tiny ears for not listening to very much

big, sad eyes

no nose for smelling or tasting

short + slightly prickly fur (like stubble)

short legs for a heavy body

big arms for cuddling

GRIEF

"Yup, that's my name, kid!" Grief said huffily. "Don't wear it out!"

"But it's such a . . . *sad* name," Leo said. "*Too* sad. Can't I just call you . . . Greg, instead?"

"Umm, I'd rather you didn't," Grief said, frowning. "It's my *name*. Would you rather I called you Lexi? Or Lacy?! Listen, let's not beat around the bush here, kid. I am what I am. I'm a very *deep* sadness. But I'm here to help you remember your Nana."

Grief jumped down on to Leo's shoulder and hugged his neck. He was surprisingly **soft** and **warm**.

"I'm sorry about your Nana. She was a lovely lady. And she made the best tuna-mayo sandwiches!"

"She did," Leo said, smiling.

He felt **happy**, remembering his Nana's special sandwiches . . . but then, to his surprise, Leo started to feel tears in his eyes, and a **sadness** in his chest that was even worse than usual. He quickly swallowed his tears down, and picked Grief off his shoulder, dangling him like a smelly sock, before dropping him on to the ground.

"Um, thanks for saying hello and everything – but can you leave now, please?" Leo said, suddenly feeling very annoyed. "I've got **LOTS** of very important things to do today."

"Like what?" Grief said, looking offended. "What's more important than *me*?"

"Er, *Lego* for one thing?" Leo said defensively. "And it's Sweets Day! I get to choose a **WHOLE** bag of sweets from the corner shop! I don't want you ruining that."

"I could come with you?" Grief suggested.

"No way! I bet your favourite sweets are things with liquorice or something gross."

"Hey! There's nothing wrong with liquorice!" Grief licked his lips.

"I knew it!" Leo said.

"Actually," Grief continued, "my favourite sweets are the same as your Nana's . . . sherbet lemons."

"**OH, YOU SEE?!** I *knew* you'd ruin it!"
Leo moaned. "Now I'm going to be thinking
of **sad sherbet lemons**, instead of
happy toffee crumble and flying saucers!"

"There's no such thing as sad and happy
sweets," Grief said, chuckling. "There are just
sad and happy memories. And it's OK to
have both. But maybe you can make some
happy memories of your Nana by getting
sherbet lemons today? She did love 'em, kid."

"Well, I *don't*," Leo said firmly. "Now
please, go away. I can hear my dad coming."

To his surprise, Grief shrugged his
shoulders and actually did *walk* away.
He went and sat behind a rose bush.

Leo frowned. He loved that rose bush. It was the one Nana liked to sniff and say, "This smells **exactly** like Turkish delight, you know!"

"You all right, love?" Dad asked, his head appearing round the back door. "I've been calling your name for ages. Couldn't you hear me?"

"Er, no," Leo mumbled. "I was . . . eating."

Dad looked at the tuna-mayo mess on Leo's plate and frowned. "What happened there? Looks like a monster's been at your sandwich!"

Leo blushed. "Err, nothing. I just . . . wasn't that hungry."

"Are you all right, Leo?" Dad said, looking into his eyes. Leo thought Dad's face looked a bit sad. In fact, it often looked a bit sad, ever since Nana had died. Leo wanted to tell him that he felt sad too. But he changed his mind. He thought it would only make Dad sadder.

"Yes, I'm OK. Why were you calling me?"

"I thought that maybe this weekend we could do something **special** to cheer you up. You know, because it's . . . "

Dad didn't finish his sentence. But Leo knew what he meant. Mum had marked it on the fridge calendar with a little flower.

Tomorrow was Nana's birthday. Of course, that was why Grief had appeared! It was because tomorrow was supposed to be a sad day.

"OK," Leo agreed, nodding.

"Great!" Dad said, brightening. "How about . . . Huffington's World of Adventures?!"

"Huffington's?! Are you serious?" Leo squealed.

It was only the

BEST

THEME PARK

EVER.

Maybe tomorrow wouldn't be sad after all!

chapter 3

Later that evening, Leo
got his rucksack ready
for Huffington's.

He was super
excited. He had
forgotten all about
Grief, who, as far as he
knew, was still in the garden, making daisy
chains by the rose bush.

When he climbed into bed, though, something big and furry was already curled up there, waiting for him.

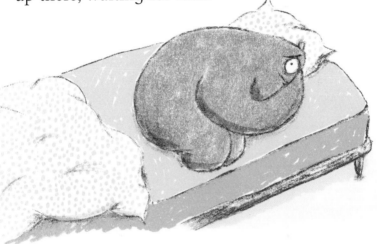

"Grief! What are you doing here?"

"Sorry!" Grief said sheepishly. "I really don't like sleeping alone. Besides, you can't just ignore me. I'm your **WORRY**, remember?"

"But you can't sleep here! My bed is tiny."

"Pleeeease! I won't take up too much room, I promise."

Of course, Grief *did* take up too much room. He tossed and turned all night and nearly pushed Leo out of his own bed.

When Leo did manage to sleep, he had the strangest dreams about **theme parks** and **monsters.**

Then, to make things worse, he was woken by a rustling sound. It sounded like someone eating crisps.

It WAS someone eating crisps! In the gloom of his bedroom, he could see someone. But it wasn't Grief, or his mum or his dad, or even next door's cat. It was a **HUGE,** shaggy creature with a leopard-print bumbag and some very cool trainers.

Leo turned on his bedside lamp, but as soon as he did, the creature ... disappeared. Maybe he'd been dreaming?

"Hello?!" Leo called out in the dim light.

"Hellooooo?"

Leo got out of bed, his heart thumping hard.

BABOOM BABOOM BABOOM.

He checked behind his door, just in case . . .

... and in the
wardrobe ...

... and under the bed.
He even checked all his drawers (you
never knew with monsters).

But Leo couldn't *see* anything.

Leo couldn't possibly go back to sleep in his bed now. He was far too worried. And besides, he didn't fancy sharing his bed with Grief anymore. So he did what he always did whenever he woke up in the night now – he climbed into his parents' bed and **snuggled** up to his mum. They had let him do this, without sending him back to his own bed, since Nana had died. Tucked under their warm quilt, Leo felt **safe** again and he soon fell peacefully back to sleep.

The next morning, Leo sprang out of his parents' bed.

"**Huffington's!**" he shouted excitedly.

"Huffington's! *Huffington's!*"

He went spinning into his bedroom and got dressed with lightning speed. He saw his bunched-up quilt and the open drawers and wardrobe doors and remembered the creature he'd seen last night. It seemed so silly now. It was funny how things at night-time seemed so scary and real. If it wasn't a dream, Leo thought, then he must have imagined it. Grown-ups did always tell him he had an active imagination.

Just then, Grief woke up. He rubbed his eyes and gave a big loud yawn.

"AAAAAAAH!"

That was when Leo remembered. Today wasn't just the day they were going to Huffington's. Today was his Nana's birthday. But rather than think about how sad he felt, Leo *RUSHED* downstairs, put some breakfast things on a tray and brought them upstairs for his parents.

"This is so **kind** of you," Mum said.

"Thanks, love," Dad said, smiling sleepily.

"That's OK." Leo grinned. He was
pleased to see his dad happy, today of all
days. He decided then that he'd make sure
Grief stayed at home. He'd only ruin their
day.

"Hey!" Grief moaned as Leo put him
on the highest shelf of his toy cupboard.
"I told you, you can't just ignore me, you
know! I'll only get **BIGGER!**"

"It's just for a few hours," Leo said. "There
are loads of things to play with in here. And
look, I'll even leave the fairy lights on. OK,
gotta go, bye, **have fun!**"

Chapter 4

When they got to Huffington's, Leo unfolded the map of the park and was filled with a ridiculous, **bubbling** excitement.

He couldn't choose which ride he wanted to go on first. There were just SO many!

He decided to go to Aqua Adventure Land first, because that was where all the BEST rides were. There was **THE SHARK**, **NIAGARA FALLS**, **THE PIRATE'S GALLEON**, and his very favourite, **RAINBOW RAPIDS**.

"Let's go on that one first!" Leo shouted, running towards the queue.

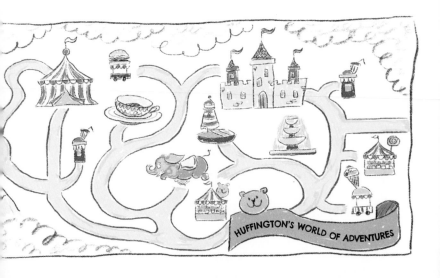

HUFFINGTON'S WORLD OF ADVENTURES

The ride smelled just how he remembered it – like **satsumas** and **cola** and **strawberries** all at once. He could see the pink river and multicoloured bubbles streaming out from all sides and eventually, when they got nearer to the front of the queue, he could see the Rainbow Rapid Dinghies! Leo had had so much fun when he was last here.

"Let's get a photo at the end, hey?" Dad suggested. "As a special souvenir."

"YAY!" Leo said excitedly.

The lady who worked on the ride checked their seatbelts and then pushed their dinghy off the conveyor belt and into the water.

"HAVE FUN!" she called, beaming, and off they went, dipping and spinning in the bubbles, grinning till it hurt.

Soon they entered Leo's favourite part – the Rainbow Tunnel – which was full of flashing unicorns and loud, bouncy music. It was all very exciting, until Leo felt something rock the boat . . . At first Leo thought it was just part of the ride. Then he saw something clambering into the dinghy. It was hard to see under the flashing multicoloured lights, but Leo could just make out a creature with lots of eyes and a long, buttoned-up tunic. He looked at his mum and dad to see if they could see it too, but they were too busy laughing at the flashing unicorns flying around their heads.

"You need to **STOP!**" the creature shouted in Leo's ear above the music.

Leo looked at it blankly. "Stop what?!"

"Having fun, of course! You're having too much **fun!**"

"It's a theme park!" Leo cried. "Anyway, what's it got to do with you?"

constantly stern expression →

← many eyes to watch out for Things to Feel Guilty About

BORING grey clothes →

notebook to keep track of Things to Feel Guilty About

GRETA
Guilt

"I'm Greta. Greta Guilt," she said, very seriously. "I'm one of your Worries."

"Oh, *great*," Leo moaned.

"No, it's Greta," she said irritably.
"Now, listen to me very carefully. When
that camera flashes, you need to look
MISERABLE, do you hear? It's your
grandmother's birthday and she has *died*. You
need to be **SAD,** remember? You can't
have **FUN.**"

"LEO!" Dad shouted, pointing to the
camera and reaching his arm out to Leon.
"Smile for the photo!"

Leo shuffled closer to Dad, but suddenly,
Greta Guilt yanked him away.

"Not too cosy," she snapped. She pulled
an ugly face at the camera and turned her

thumbs downwards. "3, 2, 1 – say *boooo*."

When they went to collect the picture, Leo was surprised to see Greta wasn't in it. There was just a big empty space between Leo and his parents, and Leo's scowling face staring back at them.

"Oh, that's a shame," Dad said, disappointed. "Let's not get this photo then. Maybe the next one, hey?"

Leo shrugged. He wished he could tell them about Greta and explain that he wasn't deliberately ruining the photo. But he didn't know where to begin. It would all sound so . . . **ridiculous.**

When they left the Rainbow Rapids, Mum suggested they all get a treat from the ice-cream stand. Leo looked at all the swirly, colourful flavours and the twenty different

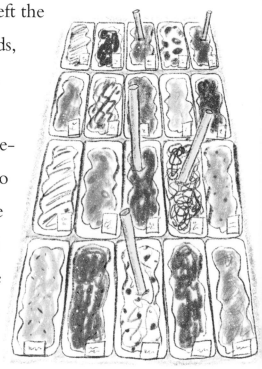

toppings. It was as if he could already taste them on his tongue, and this made his body brighten.

"OK!" said Leo happily.

Just when he had chosen his flavours, he felt something tugging at his trouser leg. It was Greta again.

"Are you sure you're going to get **TWO** flavours?" she hissed.

"Mum said I could!" Leo whispered back.

"Doesn't mean you should. And sprinkles too?! That's just *greedy*. You're not supposed to be ENJOYING yourself today, remember?"

"But . . . I'm going to share it!" Leo said defensively.

Greta folded her arms and raised an eyebrow doubtfully. "If you say so!"

Leo began to eat his cookie dough and mint-choc ice cream with mini marshmallow sprinkles. It tasted **delicious** . . . until Greta started nagging him again.

"You said you were going to *share*!"

"I will," Leo whispered. "If Mum and Dad want some, I'll let them."

"Let *me*!" Greta grumbled. "They've got their own ice cream." She took a spork out of her pocket and plunged it into Leo's ice cream. **"HEY!"** he yelped.

"One lick for you, one spoon for me," she said. "It's only fair."

"Fair for who?!" Leo said, outraged.
He started eating the ice cream as fast as he
could before Greta could
scoop it all up.

By the time he
had finished it, Leo
had eaten so fast
that he felt sick. And
then annoyed. He'd
had *such* a delicious
ice cream, but he
hadn't even been
able to enjoy it!

Chapter 5

After he finished his ice cream, Mum and Dad kept asking Leo if he was all right and if he wanted to have a rest and would he like another ice cream, **BLAH BLAH BLAH**.
It was starting to get ANNOYING.

He didn't want all this attention. He didn't feel he *deserved* all this attention.

"I'm **FINE!**" Leo insisted. "Let's just go on another ride." He didn't want to ruin their day too, so he decided he would just pretend everything was fine. That was it. Surely it'd be easy to do, just for a couple of hours.

Dad pointed to a **rollercoaster** that was swinging above their heads.

"How about that one? The Shark!" It did look awesome. Leo loved fast rollercoasters like that. But in one of the carriages that rumbled past, Leo saw a flash of something **BIG AND FURRY**. He watched the train as it slowed down on the uphill track and realized… it was the creature from last night again! And this time, it was … **waving?!**

"I'll tell you what," Dad continued as Leo stared up at the creature. "I'll just go on it and you can watch. That way you might feel braver and come on it again with me."

Leo was suddenly filled with **panic**. He didn't want his dad to go on the ride either! He was **scared** of that creature. The weird thing was, it didn't *look* scary. It actually looked quite . . . nice. So what, Leo wondered, was he really scared of?

Dad saw the expression on Leo's face. "OK, I won't go on that one then. But how about THAT?" Dad was pointing to Niagara Falls, which was going up and

down super-fast
while people
screamed their
heads off. "Like
I said, why don't
I just go quickly?
There's no queue
for that one!"
"NO!" Leo
shouted, pulling Dad's coat. "Let's just go on
something quiet. Like … the teacups!"

"Teacups?!" Dad said, barely hiding his
horror.

Mum gave him A Look. "If that's what
Leo wants, Sam …"

"Oh yeah, of course, sorry!" Dad said, quickly smiling. "Teacups will be . . . **fun!**"

The teacups were **NOT fun,** except maybe for Mum.

Nor were the Flying Elephants.

Nor the Baby Boats.

Nor were any of the other SUPER BORING rides Leo suggested they go on. He could feel the **boredom** boiling inside him and turning into something more . . . *angry*.

"I want to do THAT," Leo suddenly said, pointing to a carnival game with rows of colourful soft toys behind it.

"Yes! Of course!" his parents said, who were desperate to cheer Leo up. Mum bought him a pocketful of tokens, and Leo started to play. He **hurled** the balls with all his might but he kept on missing! Leo got angrier and angrier until ... **BAM!** He finally hit his target.

"Well done, little 'un!" the man on the stand said, grinning.

Little 'un?! Leo thought. He wasn't *little*. **UGH!** Leo felt even crosser now.

The man lifted down the biggest and fiercest soft toy on the shelf. "Here you go," he said.

Leo looked at it. "But it's only got one eye!"

The man shrugged. "I don't make 'em, I'm afraid. Take it up with the theme park manager!"

Leo took the toy **moodily,** without even saying thank you. He was already too busy looking at the next stand to see that the toy was staring right at him!

Chapter 6

"Hey!" a voice snapped. **"Heyyyy!**
I'm talking to you!"

Leo looked down, and to his absolute
disbelief, saw that the toy's mouth was
moving! Actually *moving*!

"This park **SUCKS!**" it growled.
"Let's get outta here."

"Er, and who are you?!" Leo whispered,
so his parents couldn't hear.

"I'm RAGE, of course!" he said moodily,

rolling his one eye. "Isn't it OBVIOUS?!"

"All right, calm down!" Leo mumbled.

"I HATE being told to calm down," Rage snapped. "It NEVER calms me down."

"OK, OK!"

"That TOO! I HATE that!"

"WHAT?!"

"Oh forget it!" Rage huffed.

Leo felt like dropping Rage right there and then. So he did.

"HEYYYY!" he yelped as he landed on the concrete floor. Leo's parents turned around.

"Oh Leo, you dropped your toy," Dad said, running to pick it up.

"I don't want it!" Leo said irritably. "It's not even a toy. It's a –"

Leo stopped before he could say 'Worry'.
Dad picked it up anyway and handed it
back to him. Rage turned to Leo and hissed.

"That was **NOT** cool!"

Just then, Greta appeared by Leo's side.

"What do *you* want?" Leo said. "I thought
you only appeared when I'm having too
much fun. Well, happy now? I'm having a
miserable time."

"I merely came to congratulate you,"
Greta said smugly. "That is *exactly* how you
should be feeling."

"Great. Thanks, Greta," Leo said
sarcastically.

"You're welcome." Greta smiled. "I'll be

floating around in the background if you need me."

"Oh, I'm pretty sure I won't," Leo muttered.

Leo could feel anger **bubbling** inside him again. Suddenly the noise and brightness of the park was incredibly annoying, and it irritated every part of his body. Rage was watching him closely.

"You need to kick something," he growled.

"What?" Leo answered.

"Kick something! You'll feel better when you let out that anger, I'm telling you. And kicking is SO satisfying. Look at that bin there. It's so stupid."

Rage was right. That bin was stupid, grinning

back at him like that. Whose idea was is to turn a bin into a giraffe anyway? Leo went for it.

"HIIIII-YAAAAA!"

Sadly, the bin did not topple over or go flying dramatically through the sky as he had hoped. It was firmly bolted to the ground. Leo sighed and gave another harder kick for good measure.

"**OW! MY FOOT!**" he yelped, hopping around.

"Leo!" Mum gasped. "What are you *doing*?!"

"Nothing!" Leo said defensively. He glared at Rage and hissed, "Now I feel **WORSE!** Thanks a bunch."

Rage gave a satisfied grin. Greta shook her head and grew a little bigger.

"I just want to **GO!**" Leo suddenly shouted.

TAKE ME HOME *NOW!*

Chapter 7

Leo and Mum and Dad drove back home in complete **SILENCE.** No one tried to make small talk, not even when pigeon poo splatted on the windscreen.

That is exactly how I feel, thought Leo, as he sat squashed between his Worries in the back. Greta Guilt was busy taking notes, while Rage stuck bits of chewing gum on to the back of the seats. Leo didn't have the energy to tell him to stop. He was exhausted.

When they got home, Leo was hoping to go straight to his bedroom and shut the door very tight, until the day was over. But as he was taking his shoes off, he heard his mum and dad cry out.

Leo followed the sound and peered into the dining room. There, sitting at the little table, drinking tea, was Grief – and Another Creature! They were both absolutely . . .

ENORMOUS.

Grief waved apologetically. The other creature stood up and hit his head on the lightshade, although he didn't seem to notice.

"Hello, everyone. How are you? I'm very sorry to turn up unannounced like this," he said, smiling warmly. "I'm **Death.**"

"DEATH!?" they all gasped at once.

"Don't worry, I'm not here *for* anyone!" He chuckled. "I just want to chat to Leo. It seems he's been worrying a lot about me."

"I have?" Leo said, looking puzzled.

"Of course you have!" Death said gently. "You've been dreaming about me without realizing it was me. And you kept seeing me in what you thought were dangerous situations. Like that Shark ride, remember? But it's normal. Today is a difficult day, for all of you. Your dear Nana's birthday. You all miss her so much."

Grief nodded. So did Mum and Dad. Leo was still staring in disbelief.

Suddenly, Rage marched forwards and hurled himself at Death.

"You've got a lot to answer for!" he growled, pounding his fists against Death's big belly. "Taking Leo's Nana like that!"

"SHHH," Death said gently, holding Rage's paws in his. "Let's just take a breath now." To Leo's astonishment, Rage calmed down as soon as Death touched him.

"I understand that you're **angry,** my friend." Death was looking at Leo too now. "Losing someone you love doesn't feel fair, does it? But it was your Nana's time to leave this life. We *all* have a time to leave this life. Sometimes it's painfully short. Sometimes it's rich and long. But it's never long enough for those left behind, is it?"

Leo shook his head. It definitely hadn't been long enough for Nana, even though she was 85. She had already missed his school concert, his eighth birthday party, the new season of her favourite TV series . . . He hated thinking about the **million** other things he wouldn't be able to share with her.

"Come with me," Death said. "I'd like to take you all somewhere. It's somewhere your Nana would've actually *wanted* to go on her birthday . . ."

Death smiled knowingly and led them up the road. At the top of the hill, they followed him into the small park that Nana liked to visit. Leo didn't go there often because there were no **swings** or **slides** or even space to do **cartwheels**. There were just flowers, plants, trees and a view of the town below that Nana liked to gaze at. Leo remembered tugging at her coat and asking when they could go to a real park because this one was super boring. Greta Guilt raised an eyebrow as if she'd read his thoughts. He wished Nana were there to look at the view with him now.

Dad chuckled. "It's true, she didn't really like theme parks. But she did love good old-fashioned parks."

"I wish Nana were here now," he found himself saying out loud.

"Me too," Dad said, taking Leo's hand.

Then they both began to **cry**.

Grief smiled. "That's it, let it all out. Gee, that feels **better** already."

Death watched them in silence for a while, then said. "You know, your Nana is here.

She's in these gardens, in this beautiful view she loved. But best of all, she's in you. She gave you so many memories. I want you to go home and remember them. Celebrate everything that she was."

Leo and Dad nodded and smiled and cried a bit more. Mum wrapped her arms around them both and hugged them close to her.

"I'll leave you now," Death said.

"But . . . are you coming back?" Leo asked. He had so many questions for Death.

WHAT HAPPENS WHEN WE DIE? Do you know when EVERYONE is going to die? DO YOU KNOW SOMEONE 500 YEARS OLD WHO HAS NEVER DIED? What's in your bumbag? ARE YOUR TRAINERS THE LATEST JORDANS? Do you ever get bored of your job? WHAT EXACTLY IS YOUR JOB? Have you met God? ARE YOU GOD? What's your favourite pizza topping?

But he couldn't put them in the right order in his head somehow. It was like the time he'd met his favourite TV presenter. He couldn't get a word out because he was so starstruck. Death *was* **super famous**, he supposed.

"I *will* come back," Death said softly. "Because you will think of me often. But I don't want you to worry about me too much. Worrying a little bit is fine, because it means you love life and the people in it. Think of me as a reminder of why life is so precious." Death smiled and paused for a moment. "Well, my friend, I hope that you know not to be scared of me now.

Perhaps next time you see me, you won't run away. Why not give me a nod or a smile or a special handshake, like this? **OK?**"

Leo nodded and smiled back at him. He was already feeling so much better.

Death turned and walked away. They watched him disappear.

Then Leo and his parents went back down the road, hand in hand with his Worries.

Chapter 8

Back at home, Dad had a great idea. He ran upstairs and returned with an empty shoebox and a big bag full of Nana's things.

"It's no good all this just sitting in a cupboard, is there? Death's right, we need to celebrate Nana."

Dad put the shoebox on the little table where Grief and Death had had tea.

"We're going to make a **Memory Box!**

We'll decorate the outside and then we'll put some objects and photos that remind us of Nana inside."

"What a lovely idea," Mum said. "Why don't I put on Nana's favourite music while you're doing it? I've got one of her CDs right here."

Mum put on some Brazilian music called bossa nova. The **blasting trumpet** and **brushing cymbals** and the soft singing made Leo suddenly feel happy. He remembered Nana dancing to it while she was preparing the dinner. Mum and Dad were smiling too. It was as if they were all remembering the same thing at once.

"I'm going to make Nana a birthday card," Leo said.

"Great!" Mum said. "And I'm going to make her favourite birthday cake."

"LEMON DRIZZLE!" they all said at once. Then they burst out laughing.

They spent the rest of the evening remembering Nana and sharing the memories that the objects reminded them of.

They laughed a lot. Rage eventually **shrunk** and **disappeared**. Leo felt so much better without him around – his shoulders relaxed, he didn't feel like grinding his teeth and finally, he could really breathe.

Greta Guilt was still making an appearance though.

"What's all this *laughing*?" she shouted. "Did I or didn't I tell you to stop having *fun*?!"

She jumped on to the sideboard and turned the music off. "This is far too **jolly!**"

"Says who?!" Mum said, glaring at the six-eyed creature.

"Says *me* – Greta Guilt!" the Worry snapped, hands on hips.

"Leo has nothing to feel guilty about," Mum said. "And nor do we. This is what Nana would have wanted. For us to be **happy** and enjoy our lives."

"Yes!" Dad said, peering at Greta. "Now, you can either put that music back on and join in – *or* you can leave!"

Greta looked rather **stunned**. She wasn't used to being spoken to like that. Most people just did what she told them.

To her own surprise, she found herself turning the music back on.

And helping Leo decorate his Memory Box.

She even had a piece of cake. Well, several, actually. And she enjoyed them!

By the end of the day, Greta Guilt had finally disappeared.

Grief was still there. But it didn't matter, somehow – because Leo noticed that someone else was there with them too.

Nana. He couldn't touch her, of course, but he could feel her, inside of him. And he could see her in the smile on Dad's face. He could imagine her blowing

out the candles on the birthday cake Mum made her. He could even imagine her biting into a piece and hearing exactly what she would say:

"Ooh, lovely and lemony! Best cake EVER!"

And it really was.

I hope you are somewhere nice.

Love from Leo xxx

Dear Nana

HAPPY BIRTHDAY!

I miss you every day and I wish I could cuddle you but I like the chats we have in my head.

Chapter 9

The next day, when Leo woke up, Grief came into his room and wrapped his big arms around him. This time, Leo let himself be **hugged**.

And he let his tears fall.

After that, he felt relieved. He was getting more used to crying. It had helped to see his dad cry yesterday. He used to think only his mum cried.

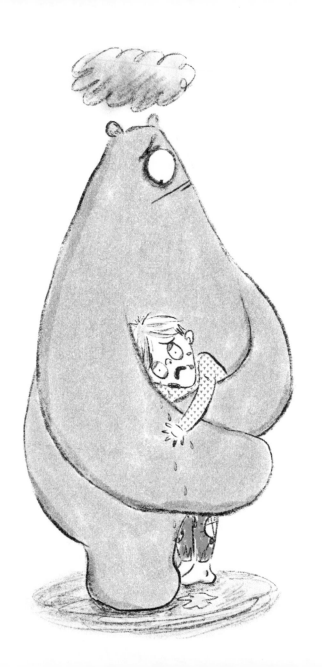

It used to feel so weird and scary to see his parents cry. For one thing, they looked so . . . *ugly.* And secondly, parents were meant to be strong. But Leo was starting to realize that crying wasn't weak. It was just . . . human.

Leo climbed out of bed and picked up the Memory Box. He looked inside and smiled.

"Morning, Nana," he said, picking up her photo. He kissed it and put it on his dresser, so he could look at it more often.

When he had eaten his breakfast and got dressed, Leo left for school. Grief went with him. Mum and Dad said it would be good for him. If he left him at home, he'd only grow **BIGGER**, they said. And probably eat all the ice cream – *again*.

At first, Leo was embarrassed. It wasn't as if Grief was small. And he could be pretty distracting. But Leo was used to being stared

at, because of his birthmark. When he was little, his Nana explained to him that people only stare because they're not used to seeing someone a bit different.

"Hold your head up high!" she'd say.

"You are brave and beautiful, Leo!" So he strode into school thinking of Nana's words. He didn't try to hide.

It felt so good to introduce Grief to his teacher and his friends. Leo felt less alone.

In class, his teacher, Mrs Rose, read them a story about a grandma who died. The pictures were beautiful and made Leo feel calm inside. Grief loved it too and asked if

he could take it home to read at bedtime.

After, Leo told the class about Death paying him a visit. Then they all talked about what they thought happened to people when they die.

Leo listened and wished he'd asked Death the same thing. But something told him he probably wouldn't have answered him, even if he had asked. Death was actually quite **shy**. And **mysterious**. He couldn't really tell which. Leo liked the idea of Nana being reincarnated though. She'd probably want to be a cute, springy dog. She did always say that she wanted one.

At breaktime, Leo and Grief played games with his friends. They taught Grief hopscotch, tag, cartwheels and clapping rhymes. Grief had never had so much fun!

"You know," his friend Simin said to him as they climbed the tree in the playground together, "I had a Worry a bit like Grief too, except mine was called Blue. She appeared after my cat, Pompom, died. She followed me **EVERYWHERE**. Even to the toilet!"

"What happened to her?" Leo asked.

"She still visits me from time to time, mostly at bedtime. That was when I used to **snuggle up** with Pompom. I made up a song about it, so sometimes I sing that to Blue. It usually gets her to sleep. Or I write about her in my diary and she disappears that way."

"Can I meet her?" Leo asked.

"OK!" Simin smiled. "When she next appears, you and Grief can come around for a playdate. Deal?"

"DEAL!" Leo grinned.

Chapter 10

The next weekend, Leo, Mum and Dad
bumped into Simin's mums, who asked if they
could organize a **playdate**. "Apparently
our kids have similar Worries," Mama said. "I
think it will do them some good!"

Mama

Simin

Mumm

Leo's parents agreed and later that day, they all went to the swimming pool, with Grief and Blue in tow. They taught Grief how to swim. And they taught Blue how to dive.

Soon, their Worries were so busy playing with each other, that Leo and Simin could start to fully **relax** and have **fun**.

Leo was pleased to see that Greta Guilt didn't show up. Not even **once**.

OK, maybe just *once*. But Leo quickly got rid of her!

LET ME OUT!

In the car on the way back, Grief seemed to be slightly . . . happier. His voice sounded brighter. He even cracked an **actual joke**!

When they got home, Grief went straight into the garden and began to dig.

"What are you doing?" Leo asked.

"I'm planting a tree," Grief replied. "The same one your Nana loved in the park."

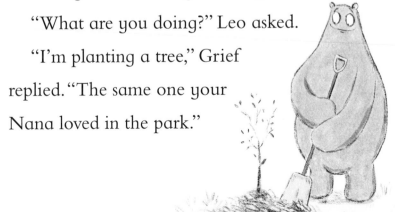

Leo began to help him. Mum and Dad joined them.

That evening, Mum read Leo and Grief lots of stories, including the book Mrs Rose had lent them. For the first time, Grief didn't ask to sleep in Leo's bed. He lay **curled up** on the floor on a fold-out mattress and dozed off, clutching the books close to him.

That night, Leo had the best sleep he'd had in a long time.

Over the next weeks and months, Grief spent more and more time in the garden, tending to Nana's tree.

He didn't get smaller. He just came into the house less and less often.

Sometimes, Leo would go out there and talk to him.

Sometimes they would walk to Nana's park together.

One day in the garden, Grief took Leo by the hand and put a **daisy chain** he had made round his wrist. Leo looked up at him and for the first time, the Worry *smiled* – a proper, **BEAMING** smile. And Leo noticed something else too: Grief's eyes no longer seemed sad. They were also smiling.

"Now you can call me **Love**," he told Leo, in the softest of voices. "For that is what I am now. I am a reminder of just how much you loved your Nana."

Then Grief-who-was-now-Love curled himself under Nana's tree and stayed there, like a beautiful statue.

Now, whenever Leo looked out at the garden, he remembered all the love he still had inside him.

And that, he knew, could never disappear.

Read on for some activities
designed with help from
WINSTON'S WISH,
a specialist children's
bereavement charity.

BEADED BRACELET

You might like to make a beaded bracelet as a way to remember a person who has died or is very poorly.

Making a bracelet is also a lovely way to remind you of the people who are around you now and who help you cope.

Beads can also remind us of happy memories, for when we are feeling sad.

YOU WILL NEED

* A selection of different beads – pony beads and beads with letters on, for example.
* Cord or beading elastic
* Scissors

WHAT TO DO

1. Think about the most important times you spent with the person who is poorly or who has died.

2. Choose a bead that reminds you of that time.

3. Choose beads for each person you want to have on your bracelet. If your bracelet is for just one special person then you might like to spell out their name with letter beads. If you want to have a few people with a bead each, perhaps choose their initial.

4. On a piece of plain paper, write about why you have chosen each bead and place the bead next to it.

5. Take a picture of your beads and what you have written so you have something to help you remember what each bead is for.

6. Take your cord and tie a random bead on to the end – this is just to stop your special beads from slipping off as you thread them.

7. Thread the beads on to the cord or elastic and remove the random bead on the end

8. Ask an adult to tie it to your wrist. If you have made it with elastic, the knot can be a normal double knot. If you've used cord, you can ask an adult to do a sliding knot so you can take it on and off easily.

WINSTON'S WISH WW

Giving hope to grieving children

MEMORY JAR

You might like to make a coloured 'Salt Sculpture' to remember the important things about a special person who has died.

YOU WILL NEED

* A small jar with a lid and a wide neck (eg. a baby-food jar)

* Salt

* 5 coloured chalks

* 6 pieces of paper

WHAT TO DO

1. Fill your jar to the brim with salt. On one of the pieces of paper, write down five things you remember about the person who has died. These could be things they liked or somewhere you went together or what you remember about them as a person.

2. Choose a different colour to represent each memory and put a dot of that colour next to each memory.

3. Spread out five sheets of paper and divide the salt from the jar between them.

4. Colour each pile of salt using one of the five chalks. Rub each chalk backwards and forwards into the salt.

The harder you rub, the brighter the coloured salt will become!

5. Carefully pick up each piece of paper and pour the coloured salts into the jar, one at a time. If you tilt the jar, waves of colour will appear!

6. When all the colours have been added, hold the jar and tap it down on a work surface so the salt settles. Do not shake the jar unless you want to mix up all the colours.

7. Fill up any remaining space with plain salt (right to the top!). This will stop the colours mixing!

8. Secure the lid and use some sellotape to hold it in place. Keep your list of what the colours mean to you close to your jar. You might like to show other people in your family your jar of memories. Can you think of a special place to put your jar?

Nana
her smile and funny jokes
baking
seaside
Scrabble
knitting me itchy jumpers

Look after myself
FIRST AID KIT

WRITE OR DRAW THE THINGS THAT MAKE YOU FEEL BETTER WHEN YOU'RE FEELING SAD. IT MIGHT BE CHATTING TO A FRIEND, DOING A HOBBY YOU LOVE OR READING A GOOD BOOK.

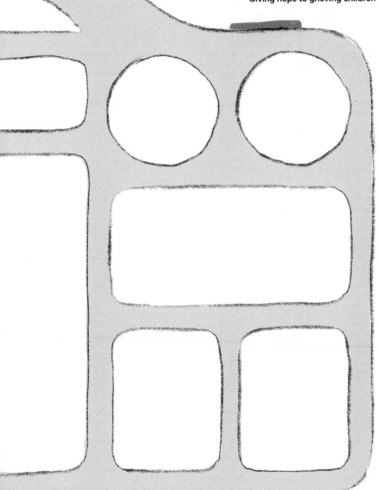

Draw your WORRY MONSTERS

give your worry a name!

FACT!
When we EXPRESS our worries (i.e. drawing, talking, singing about them), they MOVE from the panicky part of our brain (the AMYGDALA) to the calm, figuring-out part (the PRE-FRONTAL CORTEX)

20-06-23

PILLGWENLLY